Peter and the Wolf

Retold by Selina Hastings
Illustrated by Reg Cartwright

WALKER BOOKS
LONDON

Peter lived with his grandfather in a little house in the middle of one of the great Russian forests. The forest was a dark place and during the winter, when the snow lay thickly on the ground, it could be dangerous. On still nights the howling of wolves rose clearly into the icy air. But Peter's home was in a pleasant clearing. It was surrounded by a garden around which ran a high stone wall. On the other side of the wall were a meadow and a pond. Every morning Peter would come whistling down the path and through the gate, which he carelessly left open, his pockets full of bread to feed the duck who lived on the pond.

One morning Peter had come down to the pond as usual. In the overhanging branches of a tree a hungry bird was watching for crumbs to fall from Peter's hands, while an old grey cat sat at his feet, his eyes fixed intently on the bird. Peter's attention was on the duck, paddling round and round the centre of the pond greedily gobbling up the morsels of bread. He didn't notice that the cat was now lying at the foot of the tree. The bird, unaware of the danger she was in, hopped up and down on her branch, beadily waiting for the moment when she could fly down and snatch some food for herself.

Suddenly she saw her chance. Swooping down right in front of the duck, she seized a crust and flew delightedly with it to the edge of the snow-covered bank. The cat crept up behind her and prepared to pounce. In a flash Peter saw what was about to happen.

"Look out!" he shouted, loudly clapping his hands. Startled, the bird flew up into the tree, while the cat, furious, fluffed out his tail and glared crossly up at her. The duck quacked and flapped her wings and went on swallowing the chunks of bread still floating on the water.

At this moment Grandfather came striding out of the house, his face red with anger.

"How many times have I told you never to leave the gate open?" he bellowed at Peter. "What would you do if one day a wolf came out of the forest? Think of that, my boy!" And seizing Peter by the arm, he pulled him back inside the gate, which he shut and locked with a big key hanging from his belt.

Grandfather didn't know how soon his fearful warning would come true! Hardly had he and Peter disappeared inside the house than a large, lean wolf came slinking silently out of the trees and across the frozen meadow to the edge of the pond.

The bird shrilled a warning. The cat in terror leapt up the tree to sit next to the bird. Only the duck was left, and she, silly creature, lost her head completely. Instead of staying in the middle of the pond she squawked and flapped out of the water and onto the bank. In one quick move the wolf was on her. Opening wide his jaws he swallowed the poor duck whole.

Then, still hungry, the wolf looked about for more. His eye was caught by a movement above his head, and gazing up he saw the cat and the bird huddled together. But how to get at them? First the wolf stretched up the tree on his hind legs, but the branch was well out of reach. Then he tried to jump, but still the branch was too high. Finally he started weaving round and round the tree, his narrow yellow eyes fixed on his prey as though willing them to fall down into his jaws.

Peter, alarmed by the noise, then by the sudden silence, ran out of the house, and peering through the bars of the gate, saw at once what had happened. Darting back inside, he returned with a length of strong rope looped over his shoulder. He jumped onto the garden wall and from there climbed up into the tree where the cat and the bird were cowering.

Peter's plan was daring but simple. He knotted one end of the rope into a lasso. Then he told the bird to swoop down and fly about the wolf's head in order to distract his attention – always taking care to keep well clear of those sharp teeth!

The bird did exactly as Peter instructed, darting and fluttering as near the wolf as she dared. The wolf, enraged, snapped and snarled and twisted and turned, but the bird was too quick for him. While this was going on, Peter quietly lowered the rope until, with one swift jerk, he was able to lasso the wolf by the neck. The captured animal let out a howl of rage which brought Grandfather running from the house to stare in amazement at the scene before him.

At this moment the sound of a horn was heard and a couple of hunters appeared from out of the forest. They had been on the trail of the same wolf that now lay roped and helpless at the foot of the tree. Peter called to them to help him tie up the wolf and carry him into the neighbouring village.

This was Peter's moment of triumph. He led the little procession on its way, a proud smile on his face. Immediately behind him walked the hunters, the wolf slung on a pole carried between them. Next came Grandfather, his face as red with pride as before it had been red with anger.

Next followed the cat, tail in air. Finally the bird, singing blithely, brought up the rear. As the little party disappeared up the road and over the hill, the quacking of the duck could be heard growing fainter and fainter in the wolf's belly . . .

MORE WALKER PAPERBACKS
For You to Enjoy

CLASSIC TALES

THE SELFISH GIANT

by Oscar Wilde / Dom Mansell

An enchantingly illustrated new edition of one of the best-loved of all fairy tales
about a selfish giant redeemed through a child's love.

"A classic and poignant tale… Dom Mansell's delightful illustrations are
both colourful and full of amusing detail." *BBC Radio*

ISBN 0-7445-1412-6   £2.99

THE THREE WONDERFUL BEGGARS

by Sally Scott

In this colourful retelling of a traditional Serbian folk tale,
the three wonderful beggars help young Vassili overcome the cruel tyrant Mark the Rich.

"A superbly drawn folk tale … a thrilling survival story."
The Evening Standard

ISBN 0-7445-1391-X   £2.99

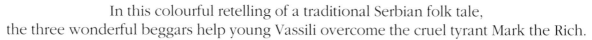

**Walker Paperbacks are available from most booksellers. They are also available by post: just tick the titles you want,
fill in the form below and send it to Walker Books Ltd, PO Box 11, Falmouth, Cornwall TR10 9EN.**

Please send a cheque or postal order and allow the following for postage and packing:
UK, BFPO and Eire – 50p for first book, plus 10p for each additional book to a maximum charge of £2.00.
Overseas Customers – £1.25 for first book, plus 25p per copy for each additional book.
Prices are correct at time of going to press, but are subject to change without notice.